W9-BRN-684

This book is dedicated to Tiger, the amazing cat who chose to spend her days on Earth with us. She loved eating, sleeping, purring, and cuddling with our daughters. Though she is gone, she lives on in our hearts. We will love her forever.

A portion of the proceeds from the sale of this book will go to The Anti-Cruelty Society in Chicago, Tiger's first home. We are grateful to them every day for putting Tiger in our lives. For more information on The Anti-Cruelty Society, visit **www.anticruelty.org.**

"This book will help children cope with pet loss and provide them with positive memories. After reading this book, I will think of Tiger, and my late pets, whenever I see a rainbow."

- Dr. Robyn Barbiers, DVM and Past President of the Anti-Cruelty Society

"*Balloons for Tiger* is a delightful rhyming book that is filled with hope. A wonderful story that can help families have reassuring conversations after the loss of a beloved pet."

- Jed Doherty, Producer/Host of the *Reading With Your Kids* Podcast

"*Balloons for Tiger* is perfectly written to help young children understand the loss of a pet and the illustrations will speak to visual learners."

- Nicole Ewalt, First Grade Teacher

"*Balloons for Tiger* helps normalize the confused, scared, and sad feelings a child may feel and be unable to express. A great tool for processing emotions."

- Jennifer Silverman, LCSW

FOREWORD

They are our fur-ever friends—the ones who purr and bark with joy when we arrive. Over the years, we are filled with laughter from their tricks and consoled by their companionship. Unfortunately, the thrill of having a pet as a family member goes hand in hand with the heartbreak of losing them. This grief might even be the first time a child experiences coping with a loss.

As you comfort your child's emotions, let them know that their feelings are valid and natural—and that you feel the sadness, too. Show them pictures of the good times with their pet and share stories of the funny moments. Most importantly, let them know that their memories will last and that they can honor their life with positivity—just as Lori has advocated within this book.

Lori and I have a lot in common. We both write books, we love our children and our animals, and we find comfort in the lessons of a good book. This book is one of those that warms and consoles the heart and instills affirmations that leave you feeling whole. It's not just a children's story—it's the perfect tool to help families honor their pet in a positive way; a bridge to overcoming sadness and finding joy with the confirmation of knowing that it will all be alright. Lori has a passion for storytelling and an unwavering commitment to empowering others with her writing. Parents want to safeguard their children from the pain of losing a loved one, and in doing so, sometimes protect them by shielding their feelings. *Balloons for Tiger* will comfort kids by showing that their fur-ever friend is safe and sound... even when they are not around, and giving them the strength to smile again.

—Alysson Bourque, award-winning author of *The Alycat Series*

www.mascotbooks.com

Balloons for Tiger

For more information, please contact:
Mascot Books
620 Herndon Parkway, Suite 320
Herndon, VA 20170
info@mascotbooks.com

Library of Congress Control Number: 2020914158

CPSIA Code: PRT0121A

ISBN-13: 978-1-64543-523-5

Printed in the United States

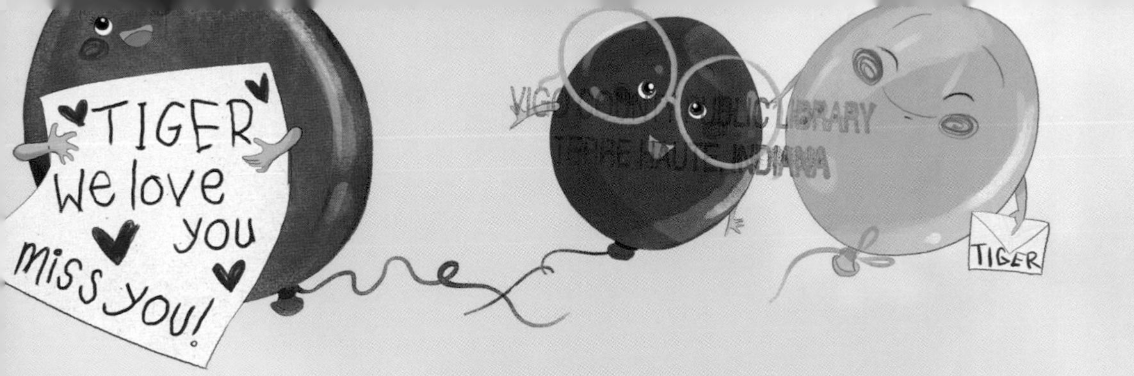

BALLOONS FOR TIGER

Lori Orlinsky

Illustrated by Vanessa Alexandre

It was a cold winter day.
When the balloons for
Tiger floated away.
They sailed off
to heaven tied
to a string.
Their parents
hoped it was
warmth and comfort
they would bring.

"Where do the
balloons go when
they're up in the air?"
The little one asked
with a puzzled stare.

Mom said they
go on an exciting
vacation.
Until they reach
their final destination!

A gust of wind pulls them over our home.
In a few days, they may make it to Rome!

They'll dance with falling leaves from a tree.
Fly over meadows, lakes, and even the sea.

TIGER
we love you
miss you!

They may tangle a bit on a power line.
But after an hour or two, they'll be just fine.

Santa and his reindeer will save the day.
Scooping them up and onto his sleigh.

LOVE YOU
YOU ARE IN MY HEART
TIGER we love you miss you!

YOU ARE IN MY
miss you!
LOVE YOU

They'll get excited when they see a giant plane.
Bound for an adventure, all the way to Spain!

They'll pose for selfies with daredevils skydiving.
And spot storks delivering babies soon to be arriving.

The Tooth Fairy will whisk past them in the middle of the night.
They'll smile for her, and show off their pearly whites.

They'll feel lots of booms and a strong vibration.
And watch the sky's changing colors in a 4th of July celebration.

They'll dodge raindrops one long, wet afternoon.
And squeal with delight when they see a cow jump over the moon.

They'll spot the colorful glow of Saturn's rings.
And catch some shut-eye nestled in an eagle's wings.

They'll watch the sun rise and set with ease.
And whirl past kites, butterflies, and bumblebees.

They'll get a wave from astronauts on board a spaceship.
Which will turn out to be the best part of their trip!

TIGER
we love you
miss you!
YOU ARE IN MY HEART

They'll hitch a ride on a superhero's cape.
And watch a beautiful constellation start to take shape.

They'll finally get to see a shooting star.
A sign that heaven really isn't that far.

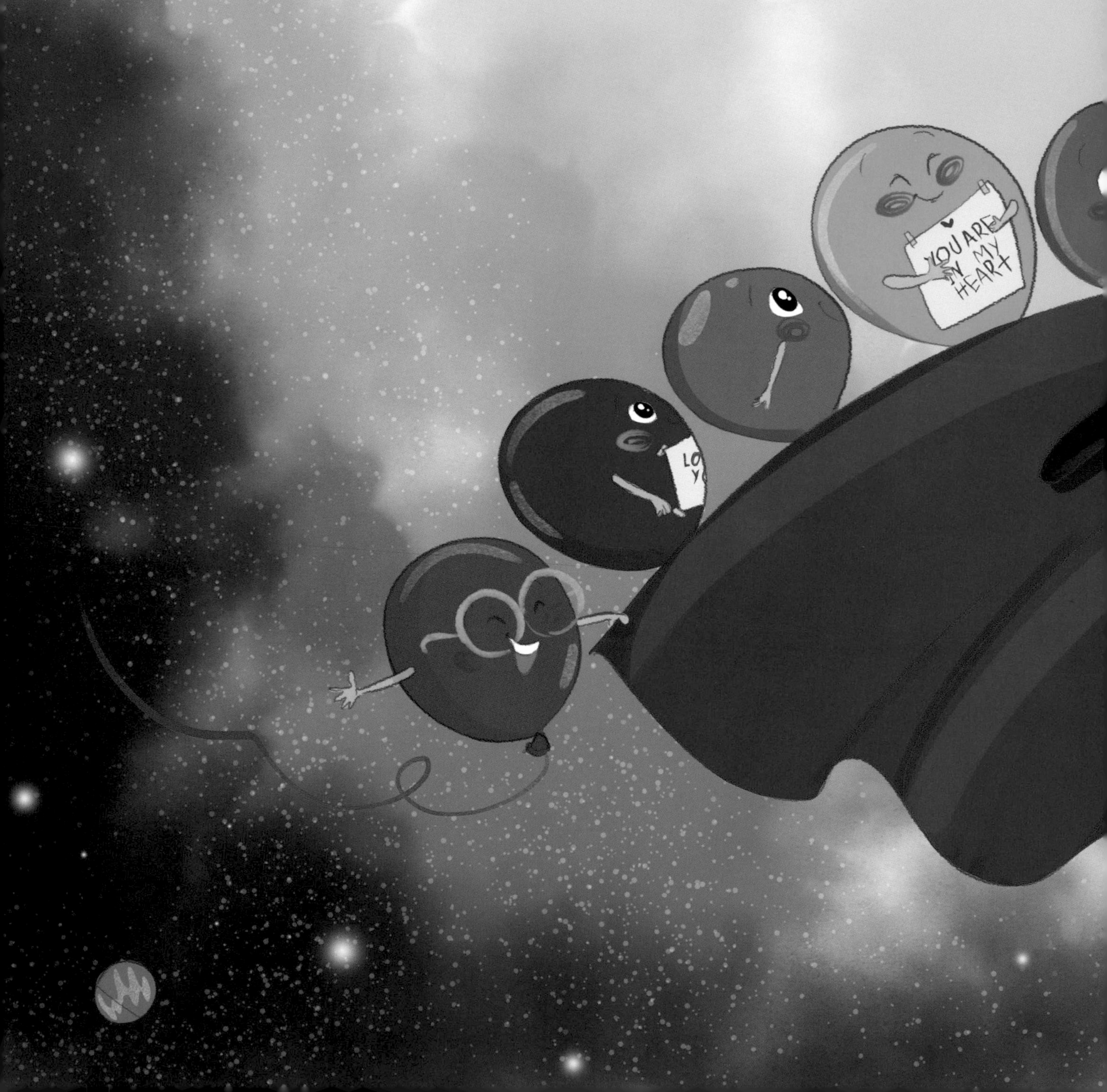

When the balloons get to Tiger, it will be sunny and bright.
After the long journey, what a welcomed sight!

Music plays, and animals sing and dance.
They bark, moo, snort, and prance.

YOU ARE IN MY HEART

TIGE
we love you
miss you!

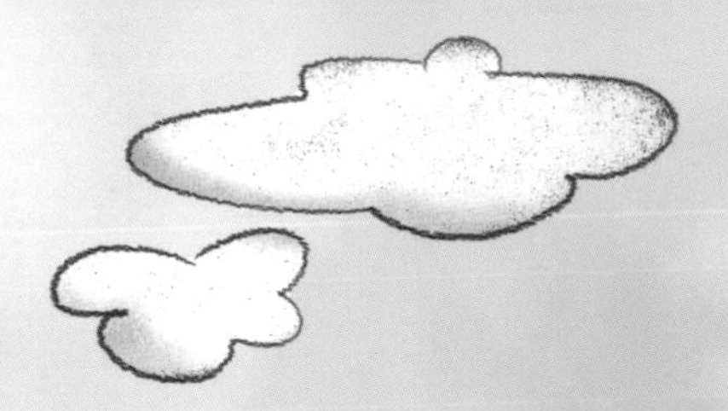

Suddenly they spot Tiger, sitting on a cloud.
When they see her, she starts meowing out loud.

She's delighted by the gift they sent above.
And makes a plan to return it with a token of love.

The little girls look up to the sky.
And it's a rainbow they spot, from the corner of their eye.

A sign that Tiger is safe and sound.
Even though she isn't around.

She'll live on in the memories in
our hearts and head.
We'll kiss her picture goodnight
when we go to bed.

Tiger isn't sick anymore, and
she's perfectly okay.
And we'll continue to remember
her each and every day.

THE END

Hayley and Ellie saying
goodbye to Tiger

COMMON CORE DISCUSSION QUESTIONS FOR EDUCATORS

Written by Nicole Ewalt, Elementary School Teacher (Chicago, Illinois)

1. What did the parents hope this story would bring to the girls?

2. What did the girls learn from this story?

3. At the end, where will Tiger continue to live on?

4. Who is the most important character in this story?
   Why do you think this?

5. How do the girls know Tiger is delighted by the gifts the girls sent?

6. Does *Balloons for Tiger* tell a story or give information?
   How do you know?

7. What can we learn from *Balloons for Tiger*?

8. How does Tiger feel when she sees the gifts?
   How do you know?

9. How do the girls feel at the beginning of the story and how do their feelings change at the end?

10. How are the girls' feelings similar to Tiger's feelings when they spot each other?

COPING STRATEGIES FOR PARENTS

Written by Jennifer Silverman, LCSW (Chicago, Illinois)

1. **Questions are important.** Make time to speak to your child, encourage his or her questions, and create a safe space to talk about feelings. Let your child know it is normal and healthy to feel sad and to miss their pet.

2. **Tell the truth.** Offer a clear and simple explanation for the loss of your pet. Use your child's age, maturity, and developmental level as a guide to determine what type of information you want to share.

3. **Memorialize and honor your pet.** Children need the chance to say goodbye. Encouraging your child to release balloons, draw a picture, write a letter, plant flowers, frame a picture, or display their pets' items (i.e., leash, bowl, collar) can provide a sense of closure and celebration. It is especially beneficial when the entire family can partake in the activity together and take joy in happy memories.

4. **Time is of the essence.** It is important to remember that everyone grieves at their own speed and in their own way. Do not push your child to talk if they want to be quiet. Simply let your child know you are available to listen when he or she wants to talk.

5. **Share the love.** Sometimes, making plans to volunteer at a pet shelter or playing with a neighborhood, family, or friend's pet can help refocus one's thoughts on life instead of death. Be careful to avoid jumping to this step too quickly as it can backfire and highlight the pet's absence instead of filling the void.

About the Author

Lori Orlinsky is a multi-award-winning children's book author who lives in Chicago. She was inspired to tell this story after her family experienced the loss of their beloved eighteen-year-old cat, Tiger. Unable to find books about pet loss to help her young kids cope with their grief, Lori wrote *Balloons for Tiger*. She hopes this book will help others, too.

***Balloons For Tiger* is Lori and Vanessa's third book collaboration.**

About the Illustrator

Vanessa Alexandre is an illustrator and writer based in São Paulo, Brazil, working as a freelance illustrator on children's books and editorial illustrations since 2007. She participated in expositions like Cow Parade and Football Parade in Brazil. In addition to her work, Vanessa visits schools across the country, performing literary activities and illustration workshops.